GODS, TRUTH, & LOVE

(A MicroSelection)

Kf.w M. Kht

1

CONTENTS

FRONT COVER ILLUSTRATIONS:

- ➤ *R.w & Kns.w (Sun & Moon)- Humans' first celestial Gods.*

- ➤ *Gye Nyame- Adinkra symbol for God's Omnipotence*

- ➤ *M'ht- Mdw Ntr ("Divine Words") for Truth*

- ➤ *Dove- Symbol for love*

- ➤ *Odo Nnyew Fie Kwan- Adinkra symbol for love*

BACK COVER ILLUSTRATIONS:

- ➤ *Nhk- Kmty.w symbol for life's energy*

- ➤ *Shu Feather- Kmty.w symbol for Truth.*

DEDICATIONS

Dedicated to my son, Tamars Gambrel, who has become a fine young man.

To my daughter Joely Jones, who returned me to her heart as her father.

To Dyquan Gibson for the many, many hours of boxing and weight training

To my children whom I miss dearly.

And to the Gwnstr.w: may I always make you proud I am one of you.

DIBAJI

When I began to grasp the infinite potential dancing between my thoughts and words, I started taking poetry seriously. I began to understand the beauty within imagery, metaphor, and simile; I started taking it even more seriously when I saw how words' spiritual movements on the page moved readers' spirits. The world changed for me during those days; it became something simultaneously magical and horrific, whimsical and contemplative, beautiful and ugly.

Someone advised me, back then, the best way to understand the value (of your) poem is to write, re-write, revise, write, and re-write it again. Afterwards, put it away. Don't think about or touch it for several years. Then pull it out. Read it and let others read it. If it retained the power that caused you to birth it and invest time raising it, and if readers, several years after its creation still found it relevant or profound, or funny, or tragic, then maybe, just maybe, it was worthy of world consideration.

And so, dear reader, I submit the following selection of poems I created between the years 2000-2021. I hope you find them as moving as I did all those years ago. If you do, then maybe, just maybe they will find their way around the world to entertain as many people as they may engage. If not, then I humbly accept they should go the way of all art that no longer has relevance to the human condition.

I present them in no particular order or according to no particular format. They are random selections that move me as powerfully today as they did when I first composed them. Many of them are Eintous-an African American form I created in January of 2000.

I sincerely hope the poems find and engage you where you most desire.

(a)Gnosis[1]

(nothing is except within awareness)

Without
(question there is!)
exist: illusory
(though as pure psyche it may be
virtual!)- a conscious
phenomenon
within
conscious
phenomena
dependent upon an
internet of minds, neural webs
of selves seeking truths their
finds may never
reveal

---

[1] An Eintou

9

Ntr

(for the misguided)

nothing is except within
awareness
the first is was
this moment of self-consciousness
when you realize everything's one

what existed before or after
has no relevance
(since that moment's wow!)
there has been no life or death
no good or evil, heaven or hell
there is only what becomes

thus who tries to name my I
misconstrues its Am
you cannot begin to know my exist
(until your flesh is no more)
upon the cross

to possess my moment
is to apprehend its now
within you
and grasp: i am not that i am
i am that you may be

USA: 6 January 2021

The mirror is blurred, and
  two wayed. Inside,
near perfection,
it is cracked along
 its rathers

Perception then- in anyview-
 left or right of it,
  seems definitive, but...
Cracked- just so- perceiving
never penetrates to truth

 Truth then, comes refracted,
  and therefore- by anyview-
  left or right of it,
  partial...
  (often undetected)

The mirror-
  long two wayed and blurred-
  is racked along its rathers
 The selves perceived-by anyview-
  see merely then, but not
what matters

Orwellian Pigs VII

(A Note For Orwellian Pigs)

("Misfortune, I am misfortune,
And my shadow has betrayed me"
                    Joseph Miezan Bognini)

These are the winter nights
 of cold betrayal we've weathered the
days
 when political phrases flurried like
sameseeming snowflakes
 and we couldn't discern from the winds
 which to taste
 which to let accumulate at our feet
 and melt
 when truth awakened our minds
 to the lies

These are the winter nights
 of cold betrayal we've learned
 to listen with willful silence
 shrouding our thoughts in ancestral
wisdoms
 as the jiggers jig master's volitions
 dancing to the stereotypical
 songs of self-deprecation and misogyny
 we've watched we've studied we

now know not all black minds think
black thoughts we
now know not all black mouths speak
black words we
now know not all black hearts seek
black love we
now know not all black bodies house
black souls we
now know not all black motion
contributes to black movements

and we
know what the ancestors wanted
when they warned
not every slave in the field
                is a brother or sister
                not everyone in the house
                is a nigger
These are
        the winter nights
womb of a new Blackness
that settles with the shadows-
studying, learning, mastering
their natures
                aborting their dawns
                bloom of their springs
                fulfillment of their season

13

We maneuver toward the hour
we can strip them of their umbra
and use it to feed our children's hunger
for revenge

Your Being Straightforward Unpoetic

You are this
epidermally contained
intramixture of cellular survival
instincts-
chemically driven,
environmentally stimulated
reactions
You filter everything
through systems of inverting and
reversing mirrors
and deem the consequence

CONSCIOUSNESS
CONSCIOUSNESS

The center of Your believing
in the myth You exist
outside Others in time and space?
Neuromaterially etherealized impulses
conducted within a jellylike,
multi-lobular, tissued spheroid. It is(!)

a cosmos of complexity
within which You maintain quasi-
awareness;

15

a Godlike, ubiquitous intangibility, the being
outside of which conceivably dissipates
the apparition You call self

Peripeteia[2]

*Right now
they are with God-
the terms I must come to;
for one of us does not exist
beyond the other's will,
and one of us
has not
yet grasped
he is just an
idea created
to indoctrine the other's world;
one of us knows his heart
empowers the
other's
spirit,
and one of us
begins to realize he's
a biblical brainfart- a sixth
day afterthought trying
to comprehend
its mind*

---

[2] An Eintou

Creative Impulse

smoking enough dope
 that grasshoppers become
asses Katy ghroppes then leap didingly
through the elephantine greenish air
(sporting tutus and boss bugging eyes)
as we exclaim
"D'you see (what?) that
Katy did!?!"

Dawning Blues

(A Blues Eintou)

it's worst
the silence since
you are gone, oh! baby
this silence is worst since you're gone
kinda like that dark thang
baby before
the dawn
before
the dawn baby
it wants to die. Oh! my
heart before the dawn wants to die
baby since you are gone
Death a' come by
and by

For Our Children

(Casualties of Black-on-Black warring)

In some unwhere
 you are spectrally becoming
 more than timespace and vibrating
flesh,
 as everso shrinking earth,
 in your backwardglance,
 and life's bittersad, fearfullyangry
concerns
 die away

Being left behind, we
 construct memorydams to contain
 overflowing sorrows rippling
 the wake of your passing

We are so engrossed by the sad
corporealities
 of this moment's silent takings
 that we fail to understand: the most
 warring souls find the greatest peace
 in resting

Neither do we fathom why
 the angels burst into dancesong
 or God,

20

in her failure to suppress overwhelming
joy
that part of herself returns,
saturates heaven
with smiling gigglelaughs

Fucked Up

Jim Beam
  beneath whose empty a
  tabletop folds timespace around
  my doobie; thisroomandi are becoming
  very Earthlike; not so much free-
  floating as we are
  axially spinning

v.o.e.l

after cumming(s)

Whrlwnds (Ii?!)
which (you in) mouthed
discharged mees, swished and flowed
rhythms- fervid, jazzlike, afric.
when I embraced your lips
(longing for some
exist),
I eyed
my closed heart, beat
and pulp reason so this
be more true than lung is breathe- this
beside ourselves panting
in purest now
lying

Orwellian Pigs VIII[3]

Urban Blues

(a suburbanite's view)

Go down
in dem streets an'
bits o' plantation 'neath ma feets
go down in dem streets, bits o' plantation
'neath ma feets. Lawd! bits o'
slave in eber face
I meets

in dem
streets bits o' slave
in eber face I meets. in
dem streets eber face I meets be mockin
me. Oh Lawd! down in dem
streets eber face be
mockin me

---

[3] A Blues Eintou

Middle Minded (a)Musings

(For Jabari & Kiri'Anna)

Early on the last day of my life's
 fortieth year, as my children,
 in bed next to me,
 sang a uniquely off-key version of
"happy birthday,"
 I reflected on roads traveled and not
 and the difference I have made
 on those taken by others

And they, disturbing my muse
 with smiles, kisses and fingers, smeared
frost-
 ting on sheets, pillows and our faces,
 instructing me:

Aging is a smile slowly working its way,
 whether we want it to or not,
 across the lips of our lives;
 and if we're lucky,
 completion of its journey
 leaves us laughing
 with the ones we most love

Rejects of the Livable City

*(to the editors of Milkweed
for Alexis Patterson)*

"We are sorry
but these poems are not right
for this anthology."
The rejection gave pause

I read it amidst evening news
reports of a 7-year-old girl
who never made it
to school one day
and her parents, three weeks later,
lose hope that their city will find her
in a livable state

Five weeks earlier,
the call for submissions posed:
"Where and how do urban habitats
intersect with and shape our lives
our sense of self and our world?"

I sent four poems:

about a city's night life
in which "life" is a whore
who screws everybody in order

to survive

about a little girl
whose brain is shattered by a
stray bullet
while her mother lays
in a crack coma

about homeless and fatherless
children who become dead adults

about Blackmen, decay
and municipal policing

But they were sorry
because the poems did not fit
into their envisioned "Livable City"

I took the rejection into my life
 where the city intersects my conscience
 and night becomes a lady who meshes
 survival instincts with diurnal decay,
 debasement, harassment, and
 marginalization

 where dawn reveals an anthology of
 homelessness
 poems rejected by compilers

of some utopian idea of the city;

where stifling the poetry of a child isn't
life's true tragedy
it's believing the work not worth
reading

I Have Known

i have known of them to dance
   my people
whether cotton picking lashes whipping
back upon their souls, or beneath
   the steeple
praying God take hold of evil
   seeping
into our world

i have known of them to dance
   the rain raining
sugar cane dance of Africa's woes,
their noses ever pointing upwards their
eyesfull tear of her years' sorrows
and always praying God takes hold of
evil
   seeping
into our world

i have known of them to dance
   my people
at the end of ropes, clubs
bullets ripping through their hopes
flesh singeing at the fires
praying on Alabama Sundays
that God takes hold of evil

seeping
into our world

i have known of them to dance the
   cocaine tango
hysterical heroine partners in the lead,
dancing
and twirling to higher worlds whirling,
tugging at god's skirt, "pray you take
hold
of this evil our world into this
   seeping!"

i have known of them to dance
   my people
the boogie-woogie, the watusi,
the lindy hop; to dance the blues;
dance to bee-bop and hip-hop; to dance
the oral mysteries of rap and lap the
spiritual
ourstories of griots into their souls
like so much sap from teaks
whose roots feed from Africa into their
energies
i have known of them to dance
   my people
dancing most when
darkness is its dourest

for it seems my people they say
the dancing dims the darkness
until god's light deems
into our world
* leaping*
leaking evil back to hell

Her Orgasms

sometimes, as she orgasms
it is not love she makes to me
she lies
immobile; her head
a backward rolling of eyes
searching for her lips-
a quiveringsweatyness of body
within which my tongue,
under engulfing and deafening moans,
swirl juices around peculiarity

she comes
to be a constriction of arms and legs
about my lower back and neck,
a Boa enrapt
twisting, rolling, wrestling
consuming its prey

disjoining her mouth, drawing me in
and pleasantly shedding all pretenses
she shrieks, my drained engorged
"Oh god!   My!   Yes!   More!"

sometimes, as she orgasms
it is not love she makes

to me
she feasts